W9-AHX-553

Manners I. Care

By

David Bruce

Illustrated by

Joan M. Delehanty

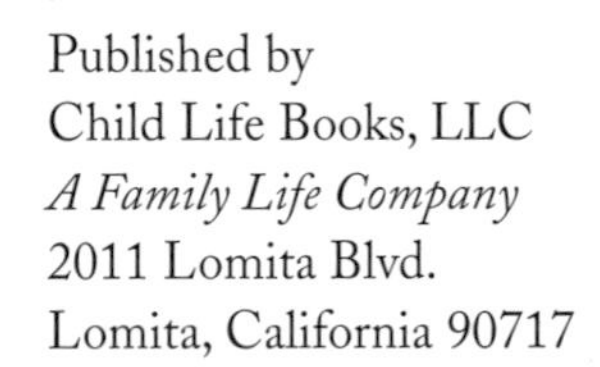

Published by
Child Life Books, LLC
A Family Life Company
2011 Lomita Blvd.
Lomita, California 90717

www.mannersicare.com

Publisher's Cataloging-In-Publication Data
(Prepared by The Donohue Group, Inc.)

Bruce, David.
Manners I. Care / by David Bruce ; illustrated by Joan M. Delehanty.

p. : ill. ; cm.
ISBN: 978-0-9771143-2-0

1. Social skills--Juvenile fiction. 2. Interpersonal relations--Juvenile fiction. 3. Friendship--Juvenile fiction. 4. Social skills-Fiction. 5. Interpersonal relations--Fiction. 6. Friendship--Fiction. I. Delehanty, Joan M. II. Title.

PS3552.R73 M36 2005
813.6/083

10 9 8 7 6

Design and Art Direction by Michael Wallen
Printed in the U.S.A.

To my Wife and Children with Love

D.B.

To Mom and Dad with Love

J.D.

You first
May I help?
I'm sorry

In Great Manners Hall, where I never have manners,
Aunt Prudy has manners all spelled out on banners.

Aunt Prudy says,

"Time out! Jack, go to your chair!"

I'm Jack, and I live in time out. It's unfair!

So what if I teased all her guests! I don't care!

A voice declares, **"Manners I. Care is my name.**

Hello. You look sad, like you're feeling some shame.

I care how you feel and I help as I can."

"Where are you?" I search for the voice of a man.

Pop! He's on my shoulder! **"Jack Bantam, I'm here!"**

The littlest man gently speaks in my ear,

"All Manners, we teach making friends who will care.

We Manners are friends, too. We help you to share."

"That fruit that you threw showed that you've got an arm.

You proved you could run when you tripped the alarm.

Two yams that you hit are smashed flat on the wall.

Jack, you're on my team if I want to play ball."

I shout, **"Thanks a lot! But the best fun I had,**
My two-twisting flip, made Aunt Prudy so mad.
I sprang from the dinner chair, knocked off her hat
And splashed all her blueberry pie around. Splat!"

He asks me,

"Who laughed when her turkey flew by?"

"Just me." I admit.

"Then please care," he says. **"Try."**

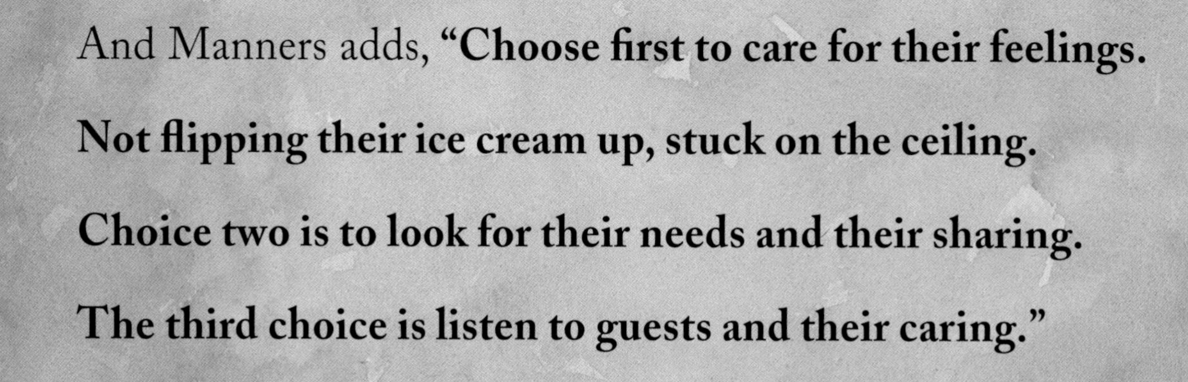

And Manners adds, **“Choose first to care for their feelings.**

Not flipping their ice cream up, stuck on the ceiling.

Choice two is to look for their needs and their sharing.

The third choice is listen to guests and their caring.”

"Please listen. No lion, no pouncing, no roars,

No parrot, no squawking, no polar bear snores.

Loud noise or good friends? Tell me which you like best."

I say, **"I like monkeys and screaming, not guests."**

"**These guests are your friends?**" I ask, "**Tell me instead,**

Just why you wear rags with a crown on your head."

He states, "**With my friends, I feel rich like a king,**

But poor if ignoring the love they can bring.

Good questions like that, Jack, are hard to ignore.

Choice four is to ask. Try to ask the guests more."

"Choice five is to share, Jack. But first try to care.

Then look, listen, ask to find friends and then share.

Just try it. You'll find you make friends while you play."

I say, **"Yes, I'll try. Here's Aunt Prudy! Okay?"**

She tells me, **"Jack Bantam, your time out is done.**

I ask you, please try to be kinder. Have fun."

Then Manners surprises me, **“Guests are like you.**

Care, look, listen, ask. You’ll discover it, too.”

Says Manners, **"Dame Louder talks louder than all**
To get big attention, because she feels small.
She cares, though. She shows it in Great Manners Hall."

Dame Louder says, **"Roses! I love how they smell.**
I grow them and pick them for sweet Uncle Mel.
When I'm sick, he visits until I get well."

Then Manners asks, **"Jack, tell me how she's like you?"**

"I'm loud," I say, **"And like attention. I do.**
But, I gave my aunt birthday flowers. It's true."

Says Manners, **"Lord Necktie is talking all night.**
He's way past their limits, but tries to do right."

Lord Necktie says, **"Yes, I serve soup to the poor,**

Yes soup, clean the tables, then scrub up the floor."

Then Manners asks me, **"How are you the same way?"**

"My aunt says I run past her limits," I say.

"I don't try to hurt guests. I just like to play.

I also like helping. I'll help clean today."

Says Manners I. Care, **"Tua Lone, on your right,**
Has four hundred twenty-two pets that can bite.
They're trained not to bite, so you're safe here tonight.
She teases her friends, but she's often polite."

She says, **"My pet Hula is cute, sneaky snake,**
Disguising her rattle whenever it shakes."

"Barmonza pretends well. My grizzly bear pet,

He plays that he's scared just to get his paws wet."

To me Manners asks, **"Have they done what you've done?"**

I say, **"When I tease too much, others will run.**

Pretending is something I'm good at. It's fun."

Says Manners, **"Those bugs are Why Me and Poor Me."**

They whine, **"No one cares!"** And they cry, **"Let us be!"**

Then Manners says, **"Ask what they like and they talk."**

Why Me says, **"We love our pet elephant Balk."**
Poor Me says, **"He's shy and, if others get near,
He hides behind drapes in the room, in the rear."**

I say, **"Both Why Me and Poor Me fuss. Me, too.
But how I'm like elephant Balk, I've no clue."**

Then Manners states,

“Balk likes to run when guests near.

Care, look, listen, ask. You will like what you hear,

When asking what guests like. There’s no need to fear.”

"Quick Kicker's a star. He defends. He can score.
If you like computers, you'll want to ask more."

"My Dad is the greatest!" Quick brags with delight.
"Why, he taught me how to make websites at night."

To Manners I say, **"I'm like him. I can't wait!**
You asked me to care. All the guests, they're all great!"

"Quick Kicker," I ask him, **"Is your team the best?"**

I ask, **"Do you score more than all of the rest?"**

I ask, **"Will you please teach me how to kick right?"**

And, **"How can I learn to make websites at night?"**

I give him a smile and he gives me his ball.

Then Manners whoops. **"Great! Jack, you shared! Best of all!"**

Friend Manners I. Care does a dance on my shoulder,

Encouraging me --- upward, onward and bolder.

Then Manners announces, **"Jack cared! That's so good!**

You did it! You looked, listened, asked all you could.

You shared, made a friend, Jack. Connecting's the key!

When sharing, you're out of the corner. You're free!"

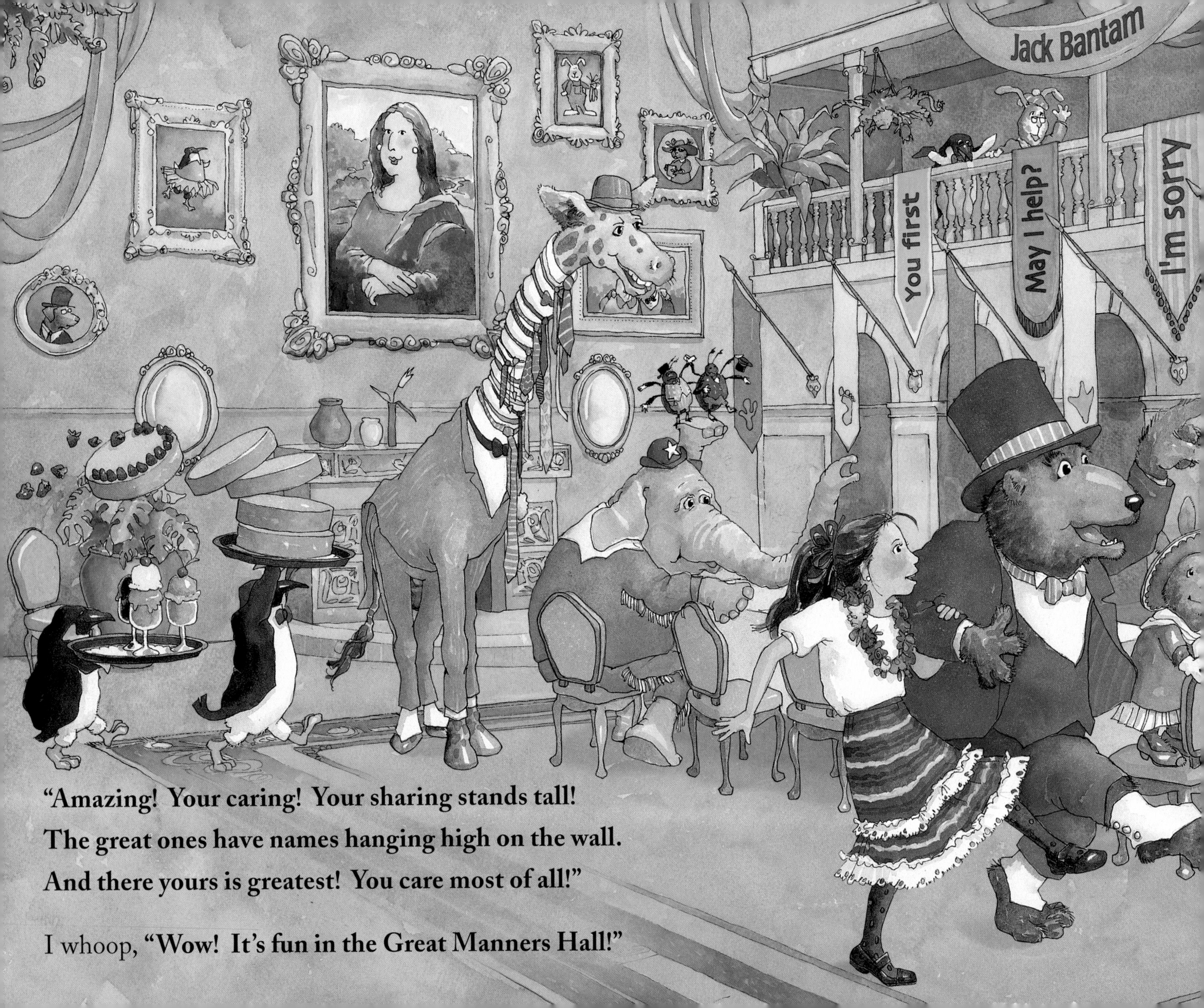

"Amazing! Your caring! Your sharing stands tall!
The great ones have names hanging high on the wall.
And there yours is greatest! You care most of all!"

I whoop, **"Wow! It's fun in the Great Manners Hall!"**

Excuse me
You're welcome
Thank you
Please

How to Make a Difference

Author David Bruce gives 100% of his after-tax royalties, up to $10 million, to charities that help disconnected kids, including:

Abuse and neglect
ADHD
Adoption
Alcohol & drug prevention
Autism
Bullies & crime prevention
Character building
Disabilities
Foster care
Literacy
Mental health
Teamwork

In the book *Manners I. Care*, the character Manners I. Care is a friend to children, a giver and a helper. Giving this book to one child not only benefits the reader, but also disconnected kids cared for by charities.

Author David Bruce says,
"I'm becoming Manners I. Care. You can too."

Be a friend.
Read values to kids.
Make the world better.
Be Manners I. Care.

To find ways you can help disconnected kids, please visit **www.MannersICare.com.**